Cool Dog, School Dog

Story by
Deborah Heiligman

illustrated by
Tim Bowers

two lions

two lions

Amazon Publishing, Attn: Amazon Children's Publishing, P.O. Box 400818, Las Vegas, NV 89140
www.amazon.com/amazonchildrenspublishing

Library of Congress Cataloging-in-Publication Data
Heiligman, Deborah.
Cool dog, school dog / by Deborah Heiligman : illustrated by Tim Bowers.
p. cm.
Summary: When Tinka the dog follows her owner to school and creates havoc,
the children discover a way to let her stay in the classroom and help.
ISBN 978-1-4778-1670-7
[1. Stories in rhyme. 2. Dogs—Fiction. 3. Schools—Fiction.] I. Bowers, Tim, ill. II. Title.
PZ8.3.H4132Co 2009
[E]—dc22
2008029398

The illustrations are rendered in acrylic paint on three-ply bristol board.
Editor: Margery Cuyler
Book and cover design by Anahid Hamparian
Printed in China

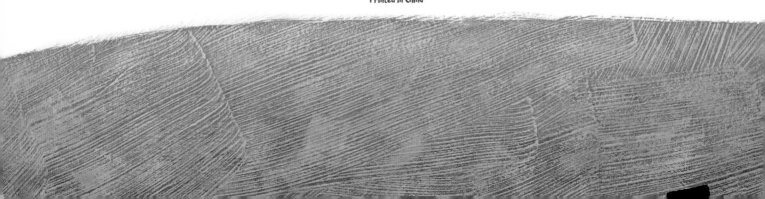

For Julia, Natalie, Amy, and Rick Sams, who were there at the beginning —D.H.

To my good friend, Joe Hickman —T.B.

Tinka is a fun dog,
a sun dog,
a run-and-run-and-run dog.

A joy dog,
a boy's dog,
a chews-a-brand-new-toy dog.

A sigh dog,
a cry dog,
a has-to-say-good-bye dog.

Tinka is a groan dog,
a moan dog,
a hates-to-be-alone dog.

A peek dog,

a sneak dog,

a spring-and-sprint-and-streak dog.

Tinka is a cool dog,
a school dog,

a breaking-all-the-rules dog.

A hall dog,
a ball dog,

a crash-into-the-wall dog.

A vroom dog,
a boom dog,
a messing-up-the-room dog.

Tinka is a bad dog,
a sad dog,
a makes-our-teacher-mad dog!

A "hey!" dog,
a "stay" dog,
a has-to-go-away dog.

A plead dog,
a need dog,
a come-help-us-to-read dog.

Tinka is a sweet dog,
a treat dog,
a-sitting-in-her-seat dog.

A look dog,
a nook dog,
a loves-to-hear-a-book dog.

a please-come-every-day dog!